NICKELODEON

SpongeBob squarepants

SPONGEZILLA ATTACKS!

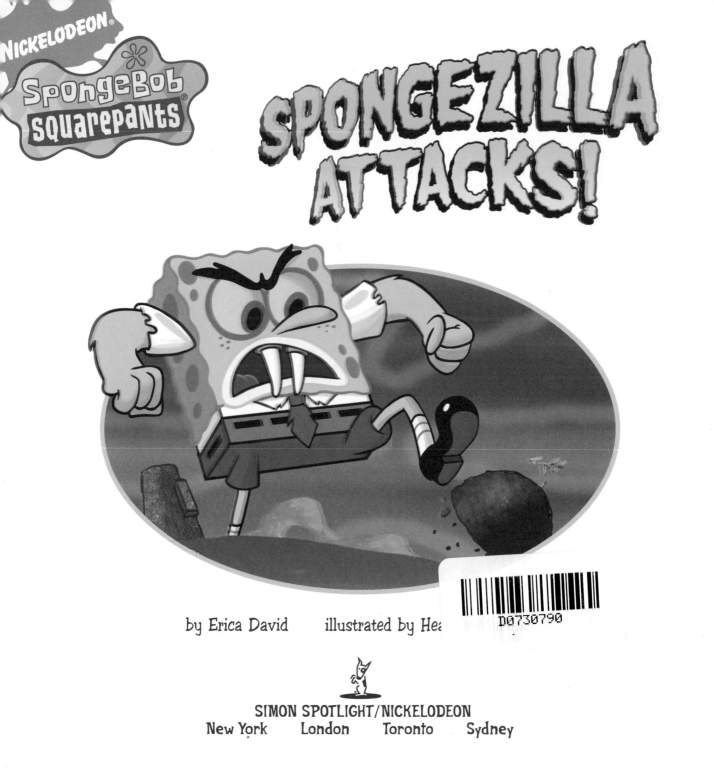

by Erica David   illustrated by Hea

SIMON SPOTLIGHT/NICKELODEON
New York   London   Toronto   Sydney

Stephen Hillenburg

Based on the TV series *SpongeBob SquarePants*® created by Stephen Hillenburg as seen on Nickelodeon®

SIMON SPOTLIGHT

An imprint of Simon & Schuster Children's Publishing Division

1230 Avenue of the Americas, New York, New York 10020

Manufactured in the United States of America

20 19 18 17 16 15 14 13 12

ISBN-13: 978-1-4169-5548-1

ISBN-10: 1-4169-5548-8

0711 LAK

It was a dark and spooky Halloween. SpongeBob and his best friend, Patrick, were watching a scary-movie marathon. SpongeBob didn't want Patrick to know that he was afraid, so he pretended to be brave.

"You're not scared, are you, Patrick?" SpongeBob asked.

"No way," Patrick replied. "Are you?"

"Of course not," SpongeBob said.

Later that night SpongeBob climbed into bed, but he couldn't sleep. His room seemed darker than usual. Eerie shadows crept across the floor. Strange shapes floated in the corners. Even Gary's gentle snoring made SpongeBob shiver with fear.

SpongeBob tossed and turned. After a while his eyelids grew heavy. He was just about to drift off to sleep when a loud noise startled him.

SpongeBob jumped out of bed and ran into the living room to find out what made the noise. He peered through the window and saw something very strange. It was a giant shiny, black . . . shoe!

Then SpongeBob heard a rumbling sound. The roof of his house ripped right off! In its place, a giant yellow monster stared down at SpongeBob. The creature roared. It reached for SpongeBob with its huge yellow fingers. "AHHHHH!" SpongeBob yelled. This was just like a scary movie come true!

SpongeBob dodged the monster's grasp and hurried out the front door.
He ran to Patrick's house.

"Help, Patrick!" SpongeBob cried. "It's a m-m-m-monster!"

"A m-m-m-monster? W-w-where?" Patrick asked nervously.

"Outside!" SpongeBob answered, pointing.

Patrick lifted his rock to take a peek. "Whoa, SpongeBob, you're huge!
I think you ate a little too much popcorn," said Patrick.

"No, Patrick, I'm over here," SpongeBob replied.

"Then what's out—? AHHH! THE MONSTER!" Patrick screamed as he
realized who was who.

Just then the angry yellow giant kicked Patrick's house into the air!
SpongeBob and Patrick ran for cover. They hid in a field of kelp as the
monster stomped past them, crushing buildings along the way.

"Have you ever seen anything so scary, Patrick?" SpongeBob cried.

"Well, kinda," Patrick replied.

"What do you mean, 'kinda'?" asked SpongeBob.

"Uh, that monster reminds me of someone," said Patrick.

"Who?" SpongeBob asked.

"Well, gee, SpongeBob, he's like a giant, angry you," Patrick answered.

"You're right! I knew it looked familiar," SpongeBob said. "It's like a . . . Spongezilla! How are we going to stop me—uh, it?"

"We should try to make it happy," Patrick suggested. "Maybe then it will stop crushing things."

"Great idea, Patrick!" SpongeBob replied.

Patrick and SpongeBob thought of ways to make Spongezilla happy.
"What makes me happy when I'm upset?" asked SpongeBob.

"How about jellyfishing?" Patrick responded.

"Right! Let's give it my jellyfishing net," SpongeBob said.

SpongeBob grabbed his jellyfishing net, and the two friends set out in search of Spongezilla. They found it in front of the Krusty Krab.

"Over here!" SpongeBob called, waving his arms to get the creature's attention. He held out his jellyfishing net. Spongezilla bent down to pick up the net, but its hands were too big, and it crushed the tiny net!

"Uh-oh, SpongeBob," Patrick said. "I think we made Spongezilla mad."
The monster roared and stomped its foot.
"Patrick, quick—make Spongezilla look at you!" SpongeBob called.
"Why do I have to do that?" Patrick asked, frightened.
"Because it's time for plan B!" SpongeBob replied, before hurrying into the Krusty Krab.

Patrick did his best to get Spongezilla's attention—mostly by running around in circles and screaming a lot. SpongeBob returned quickly with a piping-hot Krabby Patty. The delicious scent of the patty stopped the monster in its tracks.

"One extra-deluxe Krabby Patty, come and get it!" SpongeBob called.

The monster took the patty and swallowed it in one gulp. It smiled and burped loudly.

"I think it worked!" Patrick cheered.

Suddenly the creature turned and grabbed the Krusty Krab. It picked up the entire restaurant and shook it upside down over its mouth.

"Uh-oh, Patrick, I think Spongezilla wants more Krabby Patties," SpongeBob said.

"What are we going to do?" Patrick asked, panicked.

SpongeBob thought for a moment. Just then a guy in a Krabby Patty costume ran past.

"Excuse me," SpongeBob said to the guy. "Where did you get that costume?"

"Krabs hired me to wear it and hand out flyers for the Krusty Krab, but the monster wasn't part of the deal! I'm outta here!" the guy answered.

"Do you think I could borrow your patty suit, sir?" SpongeBob asked.

"Take it!" the guy replied quickly. "We're doomed anyway!"

SpongeBob put on the Krabby Patty suit.

"I don't like this," Patrick said as he stared at the crushed jellyfishing net in his hands.

"Me either, Patrick, but I'm this town's only hope," SpongeBob replied.

"No, I mean what Spongezilla did to your net. It's broken!" Patrick cried.

"Thanks for your concern, Pat," said SpongeBob. "Well, I'm off to lead Spongezilla away from Bikini Bottom before it destroys the whole town!"

"Good luck, SpongeBob. You look really brave . . . and you look good enough to eat, too," Patrick added.

As soon as the creature saw SpongeBob, it licked its lips and took off after him! SpongeBob ran as fast as he could. He ran past the boating school and cut across Jellyfish Fields. Spongezilla was easily gaining on him, though. Each step the monster took was ten times bigger than one of SpongeBob's tiny steps.

It didn't take long for the creature to catch up to SpongeBob. It grabbed SpongeBob in one of its huge hands and dangled him over its mouth.

"Spongezilla, please don't eat me!" SpongeBob cried. But it was too late! The next thing SpongeBob knew, he was falling, falling, falling. . . .

"No, no, no, don't eat me!" SpongeBob cried. "Don't eat me!"

"Hey, SpongeBob, wake up!" called a familiar voice.

SpongeBob opened his eyes, expecting to see the gaping mouth of a giant yellow monster. Instead he found himself on the floor of his bedroom, looking up at Patrick.

"I think you were having a nightmare," Patrick said.

"I was!" SpongeBob exclaimed. "I guess those movies did scare me a little after all."

Patrick looked sheepish. "Uh, yeah, that's why I came by to check on you," he lied.

"Maybe next Halloween we can just dress up and go trick-or-treating instead," Patrick suggested.

"Agreed," said SpongeBob. "In fact, I know the perfect costume!"